G. P. Putnam's Sons • New York

Text and illustrations copyright © 1991 by Babette Cole
All rights reserved. This book, or parts thereof, may not be
reproduced in any form without permission in writing from the publishers.
Published in 1992 by G. P. Putnam's Sons, a division of The
Putnam & Grosset Book Group, 200 Madison Avenue, New York, NY 10016.
Originally published in 1991 by Hamish Hamilton Ltd, London.
Printed in Italy.

Library of Congress Cataloging-in-Publication Data
Cole, Babette. Tarzanna! / Babette Cole.
1st American ed.   p.   cm.
   Summary: While visiting her friend Gerald, Tarzanna, a girl from
the jungle who speaks animalese, releases the animals from a zoo.
   [1. Jungle animals—Fiction.   2. Zoo animals—Fiction.]
I. Title.   PZ7.C6734Ta   1992   [E]—dc20   91-3368
CIP   AC   ISBN: 0-399-21837-8
1 3 5 7 9 10 8 6 4 2
First American Edition

TARZANNA!

Babette Cole

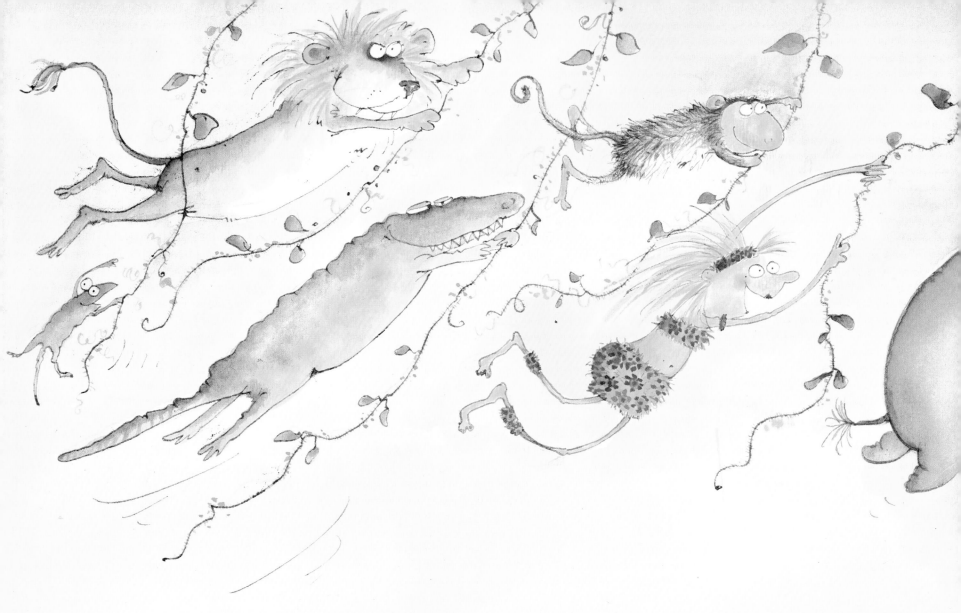

Tarzanna lived in the jungle

with the animals.

One day she saw a
new kind of animal
she hadn't seen before,

so she carried it off!

The new animal was
a boy called
Gerald.

He was studying
spiders.

Tarzanna taught him to speak animalese.

He taught her English.

"Why don't you visit my country?" said Gerald.

"O.K.," said Tarzanna.

ABC
DEF
G

THE CAT
SAT ON
THE MAT AND THAT!

ROACH!

SSSSSSSss

MEOW

Prrrrr

GRRRR

BOO!

The animals did not want Tarzanna to go.

But she wanted to ride
in the helicopter.

Tarzanna didn't like Gerald's country!

Gerald's mom and dad were nice. They knew she missed the animals, so they promised to take her to the zoo.

This was a serious mistake…

because she and Gerald
could speak animalese.
"Let us out, Tarzanna!"
said the animals.

So later, when it got dark,

that's exactly what Tarzanna and Gerald did!

They took them back
to the house…

but Gerald's mom just
couldn't stand
his spiders!

Tarzanna, Gerald and the animals ran away.

They hid out in the fanciest boxes they could find. But the snooty shoppers were scared stiff!

And so were the
pickpockets…

when they found what was
in Gerald's pocket!

"This is an awful way to live," complained Gerald. "The animals will start eating people if they don't get some dinner soon."

"We'll go and ask the President," said Tarzanna. "He'll know what to do."

But the President was
a bit tied up at the time!

Tarzanna, Gerald and the animals rescued the President.

SECRET PAPERS

"Lucky the animals were so hungry,"
Tarzanna said.

When the fuss was over, Gerald's parents
came for Tarzanna and Gerald…

…and the zookeeper
came for the animals!

"Wait!" commanded the President
in a muffled voice. "Everyone can go back
to the jungle!"

He bought them all first-class tickets home on Jungle Airways.

The jungle animals loved
the zoo animals, and
Gerald's dad built
a smashing
tree house.

"Doesn't your mom
mind the spiders?"
asked Tarzanna.

"I told her there wouldn't be any *spiders*
in the bathtub in the jungle!" said Gerald.